Rain Song

Lezlie Evans

Illustrated by Cynthia Jabar

SCHOLASTIC INC.

New York Toronto London Auckland Sydney
Mexico City New Delhi Hong Kong

To John
for all of your support, encouragement and love.
—L.E.

ISBN 0-439-13510-9

Text copyright © 1995 by Lezlie Evans.
Illustrations copyright © 1995 by Cynthia Jabar. All rights reserved.
Published by Scholastic Inc., 555 Broadway, New York, NY 10012,
by arrangement with Houghton Mifflin Company.
SCHOLASTIC and associated logos are trademarks
and/or registered trademarks of Scholastic Inc.

12 11 10 9 8 7 6 5 4 3 2 1   0 1 2 3 4 5/0

Printed in the U.S.A.   09

First Scholastic printing, March 2000

Distant rumblings

stomach grumblings

quiet moaning

far off groaning

breeze is stirring

leaves are swirling

sun is fading

dark clouds waiting

trees are sighing

birds are lying

low in nests in wait of rain.

Falls a raindrop
it goes plip plop
coming faster
drip drop, drip drop
pitter pit pat
splitter split splat

drops are falling

Mother's calling

faster, "Run, dear!"

faster, "Come, dear!"

safe inside, we'll watch the rain.

Thunder's sounding

drops now pounding

wind is wailing

leaves are flailing

lightning's flashing

trees are thrashing

cymbals clashing

big boom bashing!

Snare drum playing
beat is saying
keep the rhythm of the rain.

Music's slowing
silence growing
thunder ceasing
rain decreasing

wind is tiring

beat expiring

distant rumblings

far off grumblings

streams of light fall

birds in flight call

come and play out in the rain.

Yellow slicker
zip it quicker!
Red galoshes
squishy squashes

feet are romping

boots are stomping

puddle kicking

raindrop licking

sunshine coming

gutters running

in the distance falls the rain
far off singing its refrain.

How we love the song of rain!